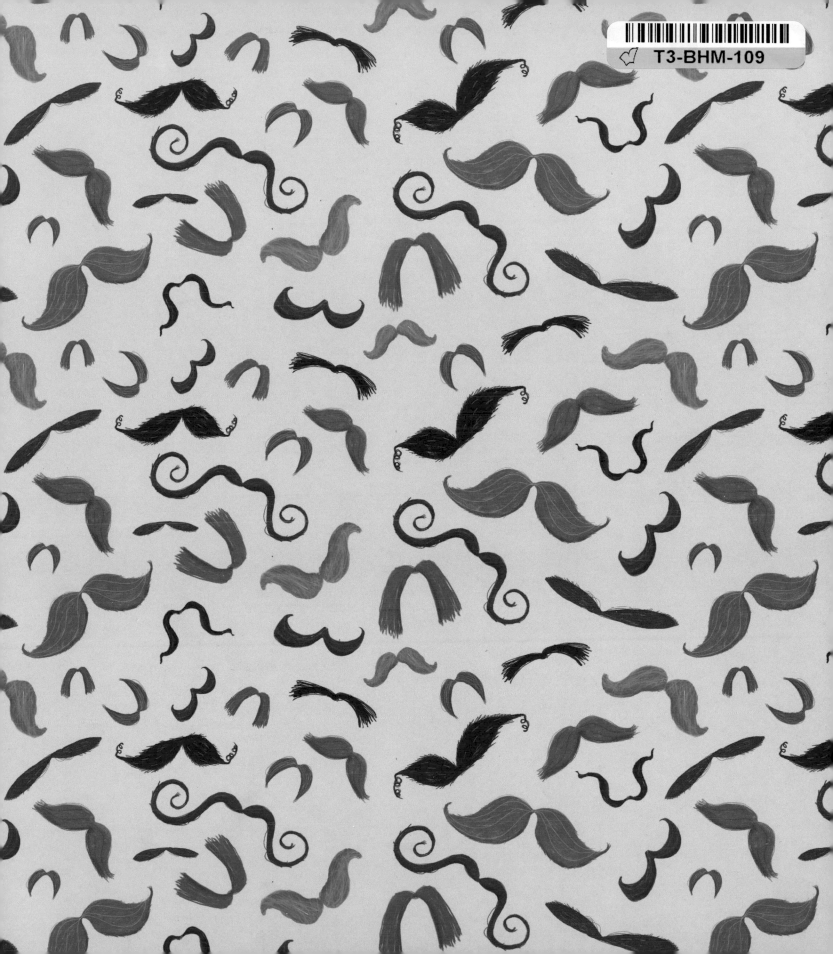

T3-BHM-109

BIG
WHOOP!

For Luca and Emilio

BIG WHOOP!

Maxine Lee

Published in the United States by POW!
a division of powerHouse Packaging and Supply, Inc.
© 2014 by Maxine Lee
First edition, 2014

All rights reserved. No part of this book may be reproduced in whole or in part, in any manner or in any media, or transmitted by any means whatsoever, electronic or mechanical (including photocopy, film or video recording, or any other information storage and retrieval system), without the prior written permission of the publisher.

ISBN 978-1-57687-683-1

Library of Congress Control Number: 2013951237

powerHouse Packaging & Supply, Inc.
37 Main Street, Brooklyn, NY 11201-1021
telephone 718/801-8376 www.powerhousepackaging.com
www.powerhousebooks.com
10 9 8 7 6 5 4 3 2 1
Printed in Malaysia

BIG WHOOP!

Written and illustrated by
MAXINE LEE

POW!

BROOKLYN, NY

Mr. Fox NEVER smiles.

He reads. He shops. He eats.

But he NEVER smiles.

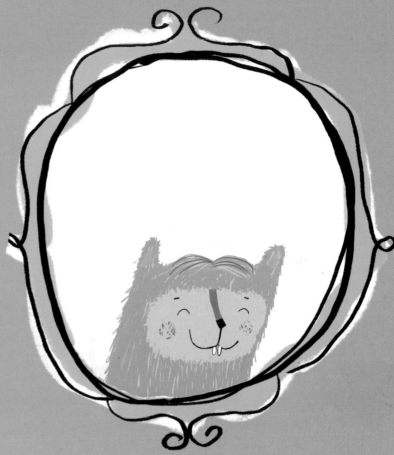

Roman and Harrison
think it's not healthy.

Roman and Harrison
have a plan.

I OPERATED A CRANE WHILE WEARING UNDERPANTS ON MY HEAD!
I rode a dragon that I tamed with my mind... and a broken chair!
BCK

We walked to the MOON ON STILTS MADE OF CHEESE!

This ant that's Crawling all over me...
Diary of an Ant
Antony and Cleopantra
ANTS ARE GOOD!
War and Ants
OF ANTS AND MEN
The Ant Games
ANTCYCLOPEDIA
Batmant
The Lion Ant
Lady + The Ant
TIME MACHINE
read 653 books in 27 minutes!

WE ARE PERPLEXED...

...AND CONFUZZLED...

...AND MYSTERYFIED...

AND HUNGRY.

LET'S MAKE HIM SOME LUNCH.
WHAT DID YOU DO WITH THAT BACON?
WHERE DID YOU PUT THAT CHEESE?
Where does this bit go?
You're standing in the jam!

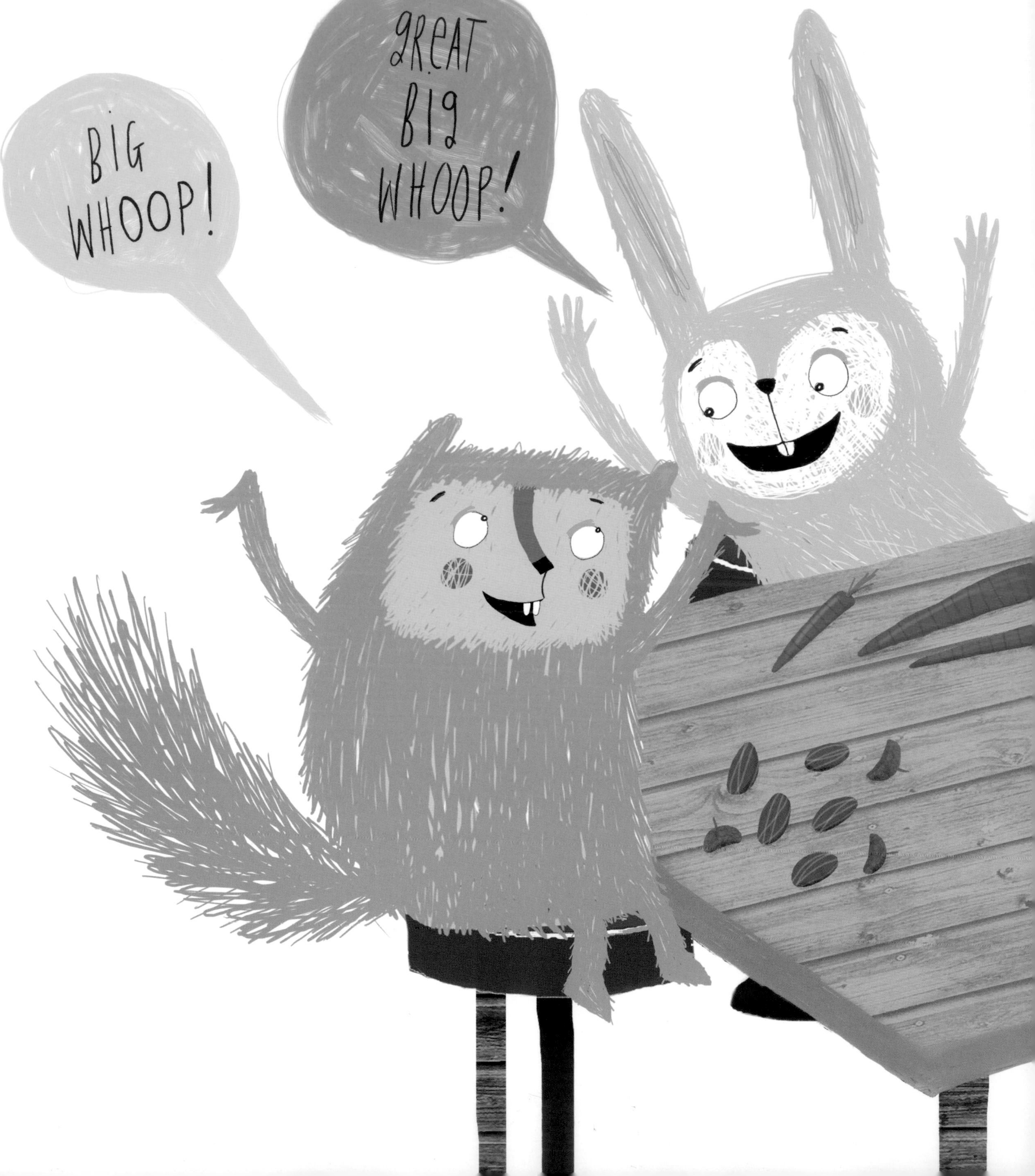
BIG WHOOP!
GREAT BIG WHOOP!